5/19 2—

W9-ARR-568

#11 Turtle Terror

Books in the S.W.I.T.C.H. series

#1 Spider Stampede

#2 Fly Frenzy

#3 Grasshopper Glitch

#4 Ant Attack

#5 Crane Fly Crash

#6 Beetle Blast

#7 Frog Freakout

#8 Newt Nemesis

#9 Lizard Loopy

#10 Chameleon Chaos

#11 Turtle Terror

#12 Gecko Gladiator

#13 Anaconda Adventure

#14 Alligator Action

#11 Turtle Terror

Ali Sparkes

illustrated by
Ross Collins

MINNEAPOLIS

Text © Ali Sparkes 2012
Illustrations © Ross Collins 2012

"SWITCH: Turtle Terror" was originally published in English in 2012. This
edition is published by an arrangement with Oxford University Press.

Copyright © 2014 by Darby Creek

Darby Creek
A division of Lerner Publishing Group, Inc.
241 First Avenue North
Minneapolis, MN 55401 U.S.A.

For reading levels and more information, look up this title at
www.lernerbooks.com.

Main body text set in ITC Goudy Sans Std. 14/19.
Typeface provided by Monotype Typography.

Library of Congress Cataloging-in-Publication Data
Sparkes, Ali.
    Turtle terror / by Ali Sparkes ; illustrated by Ross Collins.
        pages   cm. — (S.W.I.T.C.H. ; #11)
    Summary: While on vacation with their parents in Cornwall, twins
Danny and Josh follow clues to another marble but find themselves trapped
by the tide on a rocky island and the only way back is to use some pilfered
REPTOSWITCH.
    ISBN 978-1-4677-2114-1 (lib. bdg. : alk. paper)
    ISBN 978-1-4677-2420-3 (eBook)
    [1. Ciphers—Fiction. 2. Leatherback turtle—Fiction. 3. Turtles—Fiction.
4. Brothers—Fiction. 5. Twins—Fiction. 6. Science fiction.] I. Collins,
Ross, illustrator. II. Title.
PZ7.S73712Tur 2014
[Fic]—dc23   2013019714

Manufactured in the United States of America
1 – SB – 12/31/13

To Archie Evans (Read on, Archie—read on!)

With grateful thanks to
John Buckley and Tony Gent of
Amphibian and Reptile Conservation
for their hot-blooded guidance on
S.W.I.T.C.H.'s cold-blooded reptile heroes

Danny and Josh and Petty

Josh and Danny might be twins, but they're NOT the same. Josh loves getting his hands dirty and learning about nature. Danny thinks Josh is a nerd. Skateboarding and climbing are way cooler! And their next-door neighbor, Petty, is only interested in one thing . . . her top secret S.W.I.T.C.H. potion.

Danny

- FULL NAME: Danny Phillips
- AGE: eight years
- HEIGHT: taller than Josh
- FAVORITE THING: skateboarding
- WORST THING: creepy-crawlies and tidying
- AMBITION: to be a stuntman

Josh

- FULL NAME: Josh Phillips
- AGE: eight years
- HEIGHT: taller than Danny
- FAVORITE THING: collecting insects
- WORST THING: skateboarding
- AMBITION: to be an entomologist

Petty

- FULL NAME: Petty Hortense Potts
- AGE: none of your business
- HEIGHT: head and shoulders above every other scientist
- FAVORITE THING: S.W.I.T.C.H.ing Josh & Danny
- WORST THING: evil ex-friend Victor Crouch
- AMBITION: adoration and recognition as the world's most genius scientist (and for the government to say sorry!)

Contents

Dangerous Claws   11

Sinister Canister   25

Rolling Riddle   33

A Sticky Situation   41

Flipping Out   53

Net Result   65

Fat Lady Smells Funny   73

The Rocky Horror Show   81

The Scales of Justice   93

Top Secret!   96

Glossary   98

Recommended Reading   100

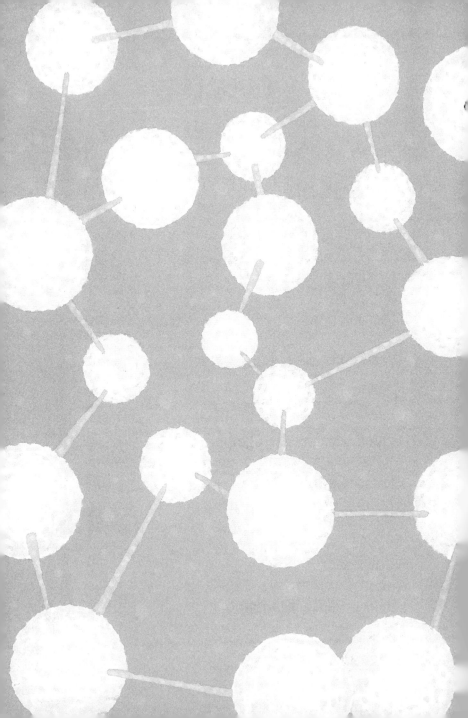

Dangerous Claws

Above the churning sea, a boy clung to the rocks,
the breeze blowing his spiky blond hair across his
face. Above him was glory. Below him was death.
Possibly.

"JOSH!" he yelled to his brother. "JOSH! Look at
MEEEE!"

A short walk along the beach, Josh was keeping
very still, watching shrimps and tiny crabs
skittering about in a rock pool. Nearby, Piddle
was licking an orange lump stuck to a rock, his
tail wagging wildly. Neither of them looked up at
Danny.

"JOOO-OOOSH!" Danny yelled. "LOOK! I'm
right up at the top now! I'm like . . . Spiderman!"

Josh sighed and looked up at his twin. Danny had been scrabbling up and down the rocky Cornish beach all morning. He didn't try to scale the actual cliffs—Mom and Dad had made him promise not to, especially while they were up in the cottage perched on the clifftop above—but the craggy rocks that rose out of the sand were just right for his Spiderman impressions.

"Yeah—great," Josh yelled back. "Piddle!" he scolded, as their terrier (named after a certain habit he had when he got excited) flopped his long pink tongue over the orange lump again. "Leave that poor defenseless anemone alone!" Above the tide the sea creature looked like a half-sucked fruit gum, instead of the marigold-like flower it would be underwater, but Josh was pretty sure it didn't taste like one. Piddle started digging in the sand instead.

Josh was about to go back to his rock pool gazing when he felt a twinge of nerves and glanced back up again. Danny was very high up this time. The rocky outcrop he had climbed was tall and jutted away from the beach and out into the sea, like a long stony finger. Danny had clambered all the way to the end, where the sea below was lively and deep, and was trying to climb over an awkward ledge and stand up on the top.

But this wasn't what worried Josh. Danny was an excellent climber, and it would take a lot to make him fall. No . . . it was something else. Something that was making its way along the top of the same ledge that Danny was about to get up onto. Something about the size of a rugby ball. Something . . . with eight legs.

Josh jumped to his feet, his heart thumping. He nervously rubbed his sandy hands through his short blond hair and squinted hard at the eight-legged thing. Yep. Even from this distance he was sure what it was . . . and that it was on a collision course.

"DANNY!" Josh yelled, running across the warm sand toward his brother's outcrop. "DANNY! Come down now! Come down!"

"Why? I'm nearly at the top!" Danny yelled back.

"COME DOWN!" Josh bellowed. The eight-legged thing was just inches away from Danny's scrabbling fingers, as he sought a good handhold for the final pull up. "COME DOWN THE WAY YOU WENT UP! DANNY! NOOOOOW!"

But at that point Danny pulled himself up over the ledge and came face to face with one of the things he feared most.

He saw eight legs and a fearsome brown face grimacing at him.

And he screamed.

And fell backward off the rock.

And hit the sea.

Danny went under like a stone. One second he was scrabbling in the air and the next his world was a blur of roaring, rushing water. Instinct told him to lock up his throat and not try to breathe. At any second a jagged lump of granite could crack open the back of his head or snap his leg.

But he was lucky—the area of water he'd fallen into was a churning, whirling cauldron, just deep enough. It broke his fall and stopped him from hitting the rocks at the bottom.

Blue-green water, particles of sand, bits of weed, and his own hair swirled around him. Danny began to struggle back up to the surface, pulling himself free of the strong undertow tugging at his legs. Ten seconds after he'd fallen in, he burst back onto the surface, gasping desperately for air.

The first thing he saw was a long wooden stick—the end of Josh's shrimping net. Josh was lying flat on his chest on the lower shelf of rock where Danny had begun his climb. He was holding the net end and waving the stick at Danny. Piddle was running up and down the rocks, barking furiously. Josh's face was white and his blue eyes round with fear as he shrieked, "GRAB IT! GRAB IT!"

As the next swell of water pushed him toward the shore, Danny grabbed it.

Soon he was back on the rock shelf next to Josh, spluttering and coughing and blowing gooey streams of seawater out of his nose while Piddle happily licked his ear. His knee was bleeding where it must have scraped against some rock, but apart from that, he seemed to be OK.

Eventually he turned to Josh and said, "Sp-sp-spider!"

"*Crab!*" Josh corrected. "Spider *crab*. Not an arachnid—a crustacean. Probably migrating right now, as it's September . . ."

"You—you—you freaky little nature nerd!" Danny squawked. "Can't you just SHUT UP for one minute about your freaky little nature nerdy facts? I nearly DIED just then! That spider . . . crab . . . tried to kill me!"

"Erm . . . no . . ." Josh corrected. "That spider crab was just out for a little walk when these huge flappy hands started whacking at it and a big ugly human face reared up out of nowhere and screamed at it. It's probably having a panic attack of its own now."

"Oh—that's right! Worry about the spider, why don't you?" Danny muttered. He could never understand how his twin brother could be so different from him. Creepy-crawly stuff just freaked Danny out—but Josh couldn't get enough of it.

"They're nowhere near as scary as spiders," Josh said. And he got up and started looking for the spider crab, much to Danny's horror. "They're amazing," he went on, foraging around the beach end of the rocky outcrop Danny had just fallen from. "They look pretty grumpy, but they're all right, really . . . Here you go!"

Danny yelled and ran back up the sand as Josh emerged from a clump of seaweed-covered rocks holding a spider crab. The beast was pale brown and waggling its spindly legs wildly, as well as fiercely snipping its chunky claws in the air. "Look at all these spines on it," pointed out Josh, grinning lovingly at the crustacean that he was holding carefully on the top and bottom of its rough, rounded body. "They call them spiny crabs too. You should see a Japanese one . . . that's huge. A six-foot leg-span, easily!"

"If you bring that thing anywhere near me, I'm going to throw sand in your face!" Danny warned, picking up a wet handful. Piddle ran round in excited circles, hoping for a game of catch, and then piddled on the sand. Danny dropped his handful and ran after Piddle. "Piddled-on sand!" he warned Josh, pointing to the wet patch.

Josh chuckled and put the spider crab down. It scuttled away noisily across the rocks and plopped into a large seaweed-y pool.

"I wonder it there's such a thing as CRUSTASWITCH," pondered Josh as he sat down next to Danny on their beach mats a minute later. Danny was glugging orange juice from a bottle, hoping the sugar in it would help his state of shock, and letting the hot sun dry out his T-shirt and shorts.

"CRUSTASWITCH?" he echoed.

"Yeah—you know," Josh said, his eyes shining. "BUGSWITCH turned us into insects and spiders, AMPHISWITCH turned us into frogs and newts, and REPTOSWITCH turned us into lizards . . . but imagine being a crustacean! If we were spider crabs we could walk along the seabed. That would be so cool. We'll have to ask Petty Potts if she can make a new S.W.I.T.C.H. spray!"

"Josh. Pay attention. I am *never* going to be a spider crab—get that?" Danny said. "It was bad enough being a spider! And anyway—we're not thinking about any S.W.I.T.C.H.ing, are we? We're just having a vacation—hundreds of miles away from Petty Potts and her secret lab and her S.W.I.T.C.H. spray . . ."

"Yeah—I s'pose," Josh said, lying back on the beach mat and putting his hands behind his head. "We probably do need a break from all that excitement and danger. Getting turned into insects and spiders and frogs and lizards is amazing—but it wears you out."

"A nice, peaceful holiday," agreed Danny. Piddle returned to his hole and carried on digging for a while before heading off up the cliff path, obviously hoping to get some lunch from Mom or Dad at the cottage.

"Yup," Josh said. "With *nothing* getting S.W.I.T.C.H.ed and *no sign* of Petty Potts and her genius experiments anywhere."

And that was when a parachute landed on the beach next to them.

Sinister Canister

For a second Danny thought it was a reckless sky diver landing dangerously off course. And then he realized he'd just gotten the scale wrong. It wasn't a *big* parachute, far away—it was a *small* parachute, close up.

Josh was already on his feet and running across to the billowing yellow chute, which was in fact about the size of a playground merry-go-round. Danny ran to it too and began to gather up the fine silk in bunches to stop the sea breeze from tugging it along the beach.

"What is it?" Josh peered beneath the chute. "A teeny weeny thrill-seeker?"

Attached to its web of fine white cords was not a tiny skydiver but a silver cylinder with a screw top, about the size of a jam jar—but much lighter.

"Aluminum, probably," Josh said, picking it up.

"Who dropped it?" Danny scanned the high cliffs above them but could see nobody.

Josh was looking around too. "And were they dropping it for *us*?"

There were very few other people on the beach. Their holiday was during school term, so no other kids were around at all—just adults, dog walkers, and a couple of surfers. And they were all a long distance from where the parachute had landed.

"Go on then—open it!" Danny said.

Josh shrugged. "Well . . . if nobody's coming to claim it, we might as well."

He struggled with the lid. It was very tightly screwed shut.

"Here—let me, you wuss!" Danny grabbed it off his brother and twisted with all his strength. Then he paused. "You don't think it's full of toxic gas, do you?"

Josh laughed. "Um—no! We're not in Petty's lab now!"

"OK." Danny gave another twist and the lid gave. Inside was a piece of folded yellow paper.

Danny stared at Josh, his heart suddenly beating hard. "You know what this is, don't you?"

Josh could hardly believe it. "Here? Two hundred miles away from home?" He felt slightly panicky.

Danny stared at the canister and then up at his brother. "*Not* Petty Potts. And now I sort of wish it *were* Petty Potts. Even if she was barmy enough to follow us all the way down here, at least she's the kind of barmy we know. But this . . ." He opened the paper with the familiar spidery writing on it, just like the other ones. "This is . . ."

" . . . from the Mystery Marble Sender," whispered Josh. "Now I'm freaking out."

Danny opened the note out and read aloud.

GREETINGS, JOSH + DANNY. ARE YOU READY FOR CLUE 3?

He gulped. "Whoever this is, they are definitely watching us. Following us. Tracking us. I mean . . . when they sent the first two clues it was all at our house and that was freaky enough—but following us here?"

Josh felt shaky too. The Mystery Marble Sender had been in touch with them over the past month, sending clues to get them to find marbles. But not just any marbles. These marbles contained a hologram and a code—just like the top secret holograms and codes hidden inside Petty Potts's BUGSWITCH and REPTOSWITCH cubes. Josh and Danny had helped Petty to find five of her missing REPTOSWITCH cubes so she could develop her REPTOSWITCH spray and they could try out being reptiles. But it seemed someone else had a code too, hidden in these mystery marbles.

What Josh and Danny couldn't work out was why that someone kept sending them clues and getting them to find the marbles.

"We really need to tell Petty about this," Josh said. "It's time she knew!"

"Yes—as soon as we see her," Danny said. "But that won't be until next week, after our holiday. For now—we've got another clue and another marble to find."

He read on. "OK—here we go:

IN THE LOW, CLIMB HIGH. IN THE HIGH, LIE LOW. AIM HIGH—SHOOT LOW!

"What is that supposed to mean?" Further down the paper the message continued.

DARE YOU SEEK YOUR DESTINY?

And at the bottom of the page was something that looked remarkably like a splodge of melted chocolate. Danny sniffed it. It was melted chocolate.

"Weird," he remarked to his brother, but Josh was staring out to sea.

"Look!" Josh pointed across the flat, sandy beach toward the water.

Danny looked and shrugged. "What?"

"All this HIGH and LOW stuff," Josh said. "That's got to be the tide, hasn't it? See the fort?"

Danny squinted at the stubby, ruined fort that sat a quarter of a mile from the beach on a tiny island of rock. It had been there for five hundred years, their dad said.

"You can only get out to it when the tide is low. You can walk across. So . . . 'in the low, climb high.' It's high up, isn't it? When you get out to it. But you can't reach it at high tide, so you might as well 'lie low.'"

"What about 'aim high, shoot low?'" Danny asked. He was getting a fizzy feeling of excitement in his belly. He thought Josh was right—and now he badly wanted to get across to the ruined fort and search for the marble.

"Don't know—but we might as well go and look!" Josh's eyes were shining—he was excited too. Even though there was something very sinister about the Mystery Marble Sender following them all the way to Cornwall, he still couldn't resist the challenge.

Five minutes later Josh and Danny were running across the wet sand revealed by the low tide, heading for the ruined fort.

With stout rubber beach shoes on, they could jump nimbly across the rocks that reared up like small islands in the sand. Danny ran up one particularly high outcrop beside a large rock pool and jumped over the edge.

There was an angry shout. He had landed on a person. A person wearing a bright orange raincoat and an affronted expression. And turtles in her armpits.

"I don't believe it!" Josh said, crouching on the rock just above Danny's shoulder. "PETTY POTTS!"

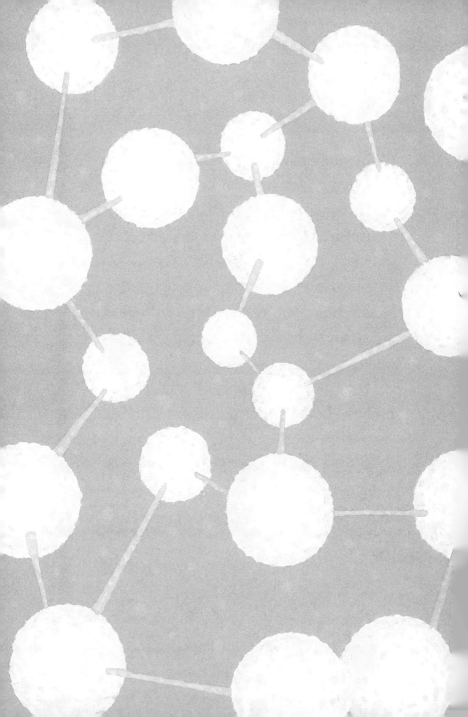

Rolling Riddle

"What the devil are you doing here?" Petty spluttered, getting up off her backside, where Danny had knocked her. This wasn't easy with a turtle in each armpit. "I thought you were Victor Crouch's government spies come to get me!" Her eyes swiveled anxiously around the beach. Petty was always convinced that the government was spying on her. She believed her former government scientist friend, Victor Crouch—who she claimed had tried to steal her S.W.I.T.C.H. secrets and had burnt out her memory—was still out to get her.

"Oh, come on!" Danny retorted, wiping wet sand off his shorts. "Like you didn't know we were here! You've followed us off on holiday before, Petty! Did you just send that parachute off the cliff? Was it you?!"

Petty glared at him. "I have no idea what you're talking about. I did not follow anyone here. I came here to do some more S.W.I.T.C.H. research, and I had no idea I'd find you two! It's a fantastic coincidence, that's all. Is the whole family here?"

"Yes—but not here on the beach," Danny said, eyeing her suspiciously. There was wet sand and a crab's claw in her gray hair. "Mom and Dad are up in the cottage on the clifftop, and Jenny's gone off with her friend Chelsea to some stupid TV show thing in Helston."

"Oh, I think I saw that on the way down here," Petty remarked. "Some gaudy yellow tent in a field and lots of people wearing yellow I *heart* DD T-shirts, whatever that's supposed to mean."

"Yeah—Jenny and Chelsea had them on! It's some talk show that Mom and Jenny are always watching," Danny said. "The audience goes nuts. It's the stupidest thing on TV, isn't it, Josh?"

Josh though, was just staring at Petty's armpits. There was a look of wonder on his face. "Petty!" he whispered. "They're beautiful!"

The turtles in Petty's armpits were dark gray
and had tough leathery shells with ridges running
along the length of them. Their legs were wide
pale flippers, and their heads were oval with dark
almond-shaped eyes and a blunt snout, under
which curved a mouth that seemed to be set in a
sleepy smile. Their shells were hard and scaly but
sleek and streamlined for fast swimming.

"They're leatherback turtles!" Josh murmured.
He was just about to reach out and stroke the
head of one when it gave a little shudder and
vanished. The one in Petty's other armpit did
the same.

"Ah—time's up," Petty said. Josh and Danny stared. There was now a slightly weary-looking black and white mouse in each of her armpits.

She scooped them up and held them both in her hands. "Well done, Hector! Well done, Percy!" she said. The mice looked at each other. Having their cells hijacked by Petty's serum was clearly wearing a bit thin by now. They'd probably been even more S.W.I.T.C.H. creatures than Josh and Danny. Danny could have sworn they both sighed.

"Wow!" Josh said. "That's the next REPTOSWITCH, then! Can we have a go? Can we?"

"Well, I must say, you *have* changed your tune these days," Petty said smugly. She put the mice into the pocket of her shiny orange raincoat. "Wasn't that long ago you were accusing me of attacking you with S.W.I.T.C.H. spray and tricking you into being my helpers!"

"That's because you attacked us with S.W.I.T.C.H. spray and tricked us into being your helpers," pointed out Danny.

Petty pursed her lips and pushed her spectacles up her nose. "Fair point," she said. "But you can't use the turtle S.W.I.T.C.H. spray today. I'm not sure it's quite ready. We can try it in the lab when you get back home next week."

"But—but—" Josh waved at the sea, an inky line in the distance now, at low tide. "It would be perfect here! We live miles from the sea! It won't be any fun lumbering about on land as a turtle, will it?'"

"Can't be helped," snapped Petty, turning her back on them and gathering up some bits and pieces she'd deposited beside the rock pool. "It's not all about fun, you know! Run along now."

Josh felt angry. He and Danny deserved a treat after all the things they'd done for Petty in the past few weeks. And he loved leatherback turtles! "I might have guessed that if we actually *wanted* some *fun* we couldn't have it!" he snapped.

"Temper, temper," called back Petty. She didn't

turn round but just stomped away up the beach.

"Wait," called Danny, waving the yellow note. "You need to know about the parachute—about the Mystery Marble Se—"

"Go and *play*!" Petty yelled back. "I have *work* to do!"

Then Josh noticed something. She'd left something behind. A small white spray bottle lay beside the rock pool—and on it, in marker pen, was the word TURTLE. Petty was heading toward

the cliffs. Josh picked up the bottle and was just about to call after her when he bit down on the words and put the bottle into his shorts pocket instead.

I'll give it back to her later, he thought.

"Come on, let's not bother about Petty!" Danny said. "Let's get to the fort and find the marble . . . and then when we see her next, we'll show her we've got a top secret code of our own! That should wipe the smug look off her face!"

Josh grinned at him. "Yes! Let's go." And they turned and ran across the wet ripply sand toward the tiny island and its ruined fort.

A Sticky Situation

Clambering onto the little island was quite difficult. It was covered in great long streamers of red, brown, and green seaweed. Myriads of little blobby olive-colored things squelched and popped when they stepped on them.

"Sugar kelp! Bladderwrack!" Josh squeaked, rummaging through the assorted clumps as if he were rummaging through bins in a candy shop. "Thongweed! Sea lettuce!"

"Josh—have you ever thought about collecting football cards instead of bits of seaweed? You freaky, frothy, frondy . . . freak!" muttered Danny. The way seaweed tickled his feet creeped him out.

"If we ever got stranded on a desert island," Josh said, "I would know which of these we could live on! And you would eat your football cards."

Eventually they managed to scrabble up the rocks above the tide line. The little island was really not much bigger than their garden back at home, and the ruins of the fort filled up most of it. Wiry sea grass and lichen clung to the ground, and a few sea birds were nesting in the dark gray stones. The ruin was a sort of very wide chimney shape, bashed in and tumbled down on the land-facing side. It was as high as their house, but there was only half a roof to it. It had narrow windows and a rough curve of steps against the inside wall.

"OK," Danny said, pulling the note out of his pocket. He read aloud, "IN THE LOW, CLIMB HIGH. IN THE HIGH, LIE LOW. AIM HIGH—SHOOT LOW! So, we got here thanks to the low tide . . . now, what about 'aim high—shoot low'? What does that mean?"

Josh turned slowly in the middle of the ruin. The sound of the sea was odd and muffly in here. The floor was uneven and scattered with lumps of fallen rock and crunched up shell and bird droppings. It smelled a bit. If someone wanted to hide a marble on the floor, it would be easy. There were loads of chinks and cracks and little holes that would easily swallow a small glass orb—it would take for ever to hunt for it.

"But . . . 'aim high,'" murmured Josh. Outside, gulls cried above the thunder and sigh of the waves. Josh's eyes traveled up the weathered rock steps built into the side of the curving wall. Some of them had crumbled away altogether, but it would still be possible to get up to the next level. "Come on!" he said and began to climb the steps, using his hands as well as his feet to stay steady.

Danny climbed close behind him, and in a few seconds they were both standing on the small area that must once have been a complete roof and lookout level. A shoulder-high wall protected them from a steep drop to the rocks below. It was like the top of a castle—going up and down in square blocks all round the wall. The lower ledges were wide enough to get your head and shoulders through. Near one of these was a box-shaped block of stone, built right up to the ledge.

"We've aimed high—we're as high as we can be," said Josh. "And that . . ." he pointed to the boxy block of rock, "is where we would shoot low—if there were still a cannon fixed there."

"What—this is where defenders fired cannons from?" Danny asked, leaping onto the block immediately.

"Yep," Josh said. "Out to sea." He pushed Danny to one side of the stone box, leaned across it on his belly, and put his head and one arm right through the gap over the ledge. "The cannon couldn't move round much," he said. "So if you shot low . . . it would be down here."

He angled his arm as if it was the muzzle of a cannon and pretended to fire a heavy ball of iron out across the waves. And then he saw it. Directly under his elbow, someone had driven a bamboo stick—like the one his shrimping net was attached to—deep into the wall, about three feet down. Hanging on the stick was a small black fabric bag with a drawstring, knotted securely into place and swinging in the breeze.

"Danny! Look!" Now Danny pulled Josh out of the way and wriggled across the ledge to see his twin's discovery.

"Hold my legs!" he yelled over his shoulder. Josh grabbed his brother's legs as Danny leaned right down off the ledge from his waist and, straining his fingers, caught hold of the stick. A few sharp tugs and it came out of the cleft of crumbly lichen and bird poo that it had been driven into, and a few seconds later Danny and Josh were sitting down on the uneven rock roof and opening the bag.

Just as they suspected, inside was a marble. A simple glass orb with a ribbon of green running through it. A brother for the red and blue ones back at home, hidden in Danny's sock drawer. Both of these marbles, under Josh's microscope, had revealed holograms of mammals and a code just like those in the cubes that Petty used to store her secret S.W.I.T.C.H. formula. This one would undoubtedly be the same.

The note with it read,

WELL DONE, BOYS! ONLY THREE MORE TO FIND AND SOON YOU WILL MEET YOUR DESTINY! SOON ALL WILL MEET DESTINY! BWAHA! BWAHA-HAHAAAAAHAHAAAA!

And under that, in pencil,

SORRY ABOUT THE CHOCOLATE ON THE LAST CLUE. WAS EATING A KIT KAT.

"It's weird. It seems a lot like Petty Potts, just messing with our minds," Danny said. "But she just made out she had no idea what we were talking about when I asked her about the parachute. But look at the evil cackle! She loves an evil cackle!"

"Hmmm," Josh said. "And Kit Kats." He screwed up his eyes and shook his head. "But . . . why? Why would she mess around with marbles instead of cubes? And if she's got some new code, why not just tell us about it?"

"Let's get back to the beach and find her," Danny said. "We've got to get to the bottom of this."

"Yes! Let's go!" agreed Josh, stuffing the bag with the new marble in it deep into his shorts pocket. They carefully climbed back down the uneven rocky steps. The ground floor of the fort seemed different. Noisier, somehow.

Danny stood still and frowned. When they'd arrived it was quite quiet—just a muffled sea noise and a few gulls, but now . . . there was a booming noise going on too. As if . . . as if . . .

"THE SEA IS BACK!" Danny yelled, running outside. "JOSH! THE TIDE HAS COME IN!"

Josh ran out too and saw what Danny meant. When they had arrived twenty minutes ago, the land between the island and the beach had been a flat stretch of softly rippled sand and scattered rocky mounds. Now . . . it was gone. The tide was

rushing inland at breathtaking speed.

"Oh no . . ." murmured Josh. "In the high . . . lie low. But we can't lie low here! The tide won't turn again until the middle of the night. Mom and Dad will be freaking out, wondering where we are!"

They scanned the distant beach and the sea all around them, but saw nobody.

"Look!" Danny pointed. "You can still see the rocks poking up through it. I don't reckon it's that deep yet. If we run, I think we can make it back."

Josh looked doubtful.

"Look—do you want to stay the night here?" Danny pointed at the dark looming ruin behind them, and Josh shuddered. He did not.

"OK, then—let's go!" he said.

They started running, slithering down across the seaweed-y rocks, and by the time they got onto the sandy seabed the water was up to their knees. Josh felt a stab of anxiety, but Danny just ran ahead, splashing sea water high in the air and soaking his shorts. "Come ON!" he called back. "We haven't got much time!"

They were only halfway back when Josh realized their mistake. On a large flat beach like this, they couldn't outrun the sea. One minute he was splashing along up to his knees—the next he was wading up to his waist, and the next, the water was up to his chest. He glanced across to Danny and saw his brother was swimming.

"We can do this!" he shouted, but he sounded as scared as Josh felt.

Although Danny was super sporty, he'd never really gotten into swimming—and Josh wasn't sporty at all and hadn't swum even half as much as Danny. Even so, they probably would have been all right . . . except for the undertow.

The current of water that pulled away from the

shore every time the waves receded was incredibly strong. Danny felt as if the sea had grabbed him by the legs and was tugging him backward. And he wasn't getting any closer to the shore.

"We're not going to make it!" spluttered Danny. "We'll have to go back to the fort!"

But as he turned his head he realized, with horror, that the fort was no longer behind them. In their struggles with the tide, they had been swept along the beach, and the fort was far, far away. They had no more hope of reaching the fort than they had of reaching the beach.

Things were looking bad.

Very bad.

Flipping Out

Josh went under. A big slap of salty water engulfed his head, and his ears immediately filled up with sea, all booming and glugging and weird. But even underwater, he had a brilliant idea. When his head next surfaced, he was holding something up out of the water with his right hand: a small white spray bottle. The first thing he did was spray Danny, whose panicky head was bobbing close by.

The next thing he did was go under the water again, with a splutter. Then, as soon as he managed to push back up above the waves, gasping for air, he sprayed the bottle at his own head and quickly shoved it back deep into his shorts pocket. Danny had already vanished, and Josh was praying he'd been S.W.I.T.C.H.ed—not drowned.

Three seconds later he found out.

The hostile world of the rising tide suddenly changed miraculously to a brand new universe. He was underwater, swimming almost effortlessly with four flippers perfectly designed for the job. His nostrils clamped tightly shut and his eyes opened wide. There was no need to swim up and gasp for air—he had plenty stored inside his lungs. He could dive down a mile deep if he needed to.

Thanks, Petty! he thought. *This time you've definitely saved my life!* But what about Danny? Suddenly he felt panicked. Had he managed to get the S.W.I.T.C.H. spray onto Danny's head? What if the sea breeze had blown it away before it could hit? Where was Danny? Where was he?

"YAAAAAAAAAAAAAY!" Suddenly a handsome leatherback turtle shot past him in a plume of bubbles. "WOOOOOOOOOOOOOW!" went on Danny. "How did *that* happen?"

Josh turned easily in the water and took in his brother's sleek reptile form. "Um . . . I kind of . . . stole Petty's S.W.I.T.C.H. spray," he admitted.

In the shafts of summer sun that broke through the greenish-blue water, Danny could see his

brother's guilty grin. "*You!*" he chortled. "*A thief?* Never!"

"Well . . . I more sort of . . . borrowed it," Josh said. "I was going to give it back to her. She left it behind. In a way."

Danny swam across to his brother with two easy pushes of his powerful back flippers and high-fived him with a front flipper. "Well, I don't mind your new crime habit—not when it's just saved our lives! And this is *fantastic!* I love being a turtle! I can really swim! And breathe underwater! How cool is *that?*"

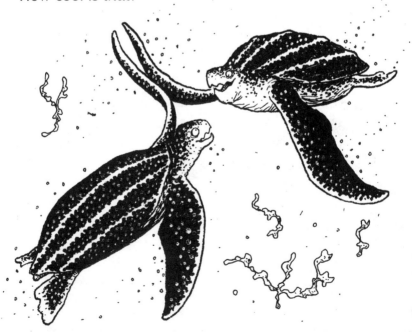

"Well, you're not actually breathing underwater," Josh said. "You're just holding your breath—you haven't got gills or anything."

"It doesn't feel like I'm holding my breath," Danny said as they smoothly navigated past a little uprising of rock and wafting seaweed.

"Well—no, it won't for a bit," Josh said. "Leatherback turtles can hold their breath for half an hour. We've only been under a couple of minutes. You won't notice you need more air for ages yet."

"And we're talking too—how's that working? Vibrations again?"

"Yep—like when we were frogs. And body language—and maybe a bit of telepathy," Josh guessed.

"Right—so—let's get down to the nitty-gritty," Danny said. "Can anything eat me?"

Josh flippered right up and over in a joyful somersault. "Nothing!" he cried. "Not around here! If we were in another part of the world, a crocodile might have a go—and humans, of course. Turtle tastes pretty good. But here we're protected!"

Danny did a twisting roll of delight as they traveled on at high speed, barely troubled by the continual push and pull of the tide. "I love conservationists!"

Josh swam down low to inspect the seabed. The sand between the rocks lay in tiny undulating dunes, forever shifting and sifting with the movement of the water. On the rocks, seaweed waved back and forth in a multitude of colors—much more vivid than when it was slumped and still at low tide. Pink and blue sea anemones thrust out their pointed tentacles and joined in the dance. Delicate, semitransparent shrimps foraged among them. Crabs traveled sideways along the sand, moving like astronauts in zero gravity and busily flicking their little mouth parts. They didn't seem to be scared of the huge leatherback turtles. And Josh

and Danny were huge! About three feet long from snout to tail, Josh reckoned—much bigger than the turtles the mice had S.W.I.T.C.H.ed into. Maybe it was because he and Danny had been bigger to start with . . . or maybe the bottle he had "borrowed" had a slightly different S.W.I.T.C.H. in it. Josh didn't really care. The water felt cool, silky, and comfortable— and it was amazing to be able to power through whenever he felt the urge. "Look at this, Danny!" he called over his leathery shoulder. "Look!" And he shot across the seabed at great speed.

Seconds later Danny had caught up with him, his flippers working brilliantly, driving him through the water. He was very competitive and couldn't bear to be left behind. "This is the best S.W.I.T.C.H. we've *ever* had!" he said. "I can't believe Petty didn't want us to do this. It's brilliant!"

"You know . . . we're actually dinosaurs," Josh said.

"We what?" Danny flipped round again and stared at his brother in fascination.

"Yup—we date right back to the Cretaceous period," Josh said proudly.

"For once, freaky little nature nerd—that's quite cool!" Danny admitted. "Best S.W.I.T.C.H. ever," he murmured, again.

"We'd better not get too far out," Josh warned. "We don't know when it'll wear off. We ought to head for the shore."

They turned toward the beach. They didn't need to bob up out of the water to check the direction—they seemed to have an internal compass that just told them where to go.

"I'm hungry," Danny said. And he turned and shot sideways toward a small pulsing cloud that was drifting through the water. Josh knew what it was immediately, but he wondered whether he should tell Danny. His brother had a habit of eating stuff while S.W.I.T.C.H.ed that freaked him out later when he S.W.I.T.C.H.ed back again.

But Danny was already swimming into the cloud of delicate white parachutes with see-through bodies pulsating through the water. Before Josh could say anything, he opened his mouth and slurped one in. It struggled briefly in his throat but could not escape. Josh knew this was because his brother's reptilian throat had backward-facing spines to prevent his lunch from swimming back up it again.

"What does it taste like?" he asked Danny as the living cloud scattered and swam away fast.

"Um . . . what? The . . . sea jelly?" Danny asked, after a gulp.

"Yes . . . the 'sea jelly,'" Josh said, making air-quote movements with his flippers. "What's it like?"

"Well . . . quite nice," Danny said. He started to look a little sick. "I . . . just ate something icky, didn't I?"

"Not for a turtle," Josh said. "It's turtle takeout, that is. You ate a jellyfish."

"Eeeeurgh!" Danny said. "Why did you let me do that?"

"Well . . . you said you were hungry!" Josh shrugged and laughed. "And that's what leatherback turtles eat. That reminds me," he added as he and his brother swam on toward the shallows. "There *is* something that can kill you here."

"What?" Danny spun round, making a small vortex of sand and bits of floating seaweed. "A shark? A whale?"

"Far worse than that," said Josh. "A plastic bag."

Danny cuffed his brother's gray, white, and beige patterned head with one flipper. "You really had me worried there!"

"Well, you *should* be worried if you're going to swim around scarfing stuff without checking what it is first," Josh said. "Hundreds of leatherbacks die every year because they've mistaken a plastic bag for a jellyfish. Floating in the water they look really similar. The plastic bag blocks up their insides and stops other food from getting through. It makes them starve."

Danny grimaced. "Um . . . that *was* actually a jellyfish I ate, wasn't it?"

"Yes—it was," confirmed Josh.

"Phew!"

They coasted over some rocks and stumps of old wood. And then Josh stopped. Very abruptly. He had not intended to stop. Something had stopped *him*.

And that something was not planning to ever let him go . . .

Net Result

For a few seconds Danny didn't even notice. He swam on toward the beach, loving the way the sunlight dappled down through the warm waves and made ever-shifting patterns across the seabed. And he still hadn't even needed to take a breath! This was so amazing! He and Josh should just forget about giving the S.W.I.T.C.H. spray back to Petty and keep it all week. They could swim out in the sea every day—maybe even go offshore for miles and swim down to explore wrecks!

He started to say this to his brother—and then he noticed that his brother wasn't next to him. Or behind him. Or anywhere.

"Josh? Josh? Where are you?" He waited, effortlessly treading water as his call traveled through the sea. At first he heard nothing . . .

and then . . . a kind of squeak. He flipped round and swam straight for the source of the squeak. He still couldn't see Josh, though, and now his heart began to skip about, rather fast. What had happened? Had Josh S.W.I.T.C.H.ed back to a boy already? That could mean trouble.

Josh had not S.W.I.T.C.H.ed back, but he was still in trouble. He was trapped.

He hadn't seen it because it was pale and almost transparent. But the abandoned fishing net had wrapped itself around him as if it was a living predator. He had swum right into it and become entangled in moments. Part of the net was firmly anchored in some rocks. In its frayed grip were several dead creatures—some fish and some crabs. They had tried to escape and failed. But surely he, a great big strong leatherback turtle, could get out of this? It was only after he'd tried—and then tried some more, and then some more, flapping about more and more agitatedly— that he started shouting for Danny.

At last Danny came back for him. "What have you gone and done?" He chuckled and started

trying to unravel the netting from his brother's
flippers, shell, and head. But all too soon he
realized that he couldn't do it. The more he tried
to unravel Josh, the more the net seemed to
tangle and snag and tighten.

"Stop!" Josh yelled, eventually. "You'll end up
getting caught in it too!"

"I'll bite through it!" Danny said and went to
snap his mouth on the thin, strong fibers. But it
was no good. He had only one pointed sort of
tooth at the front of his mouth—all the other
spiky "teeth" were right down in his throat. He
just wasn't designed for gnawing.

"Josh!" he puffed, feeling really scared now. "You've got to get out of there!"

"Yessss," Josh said. "I had worked that out!"

"We could S.W.I.T.C.H. back at any time now!" Danny said, slapping his front flipper against his scaly forehead.

"Well done for reminding me!" Josh glared at him balefully through the criss-cross net.

"But if you S.W.I.T.C.H. back still stuck down here, you'll have to breathe right away!"

"Correct! Have a gold star!"

"And then you won't be able to, and . . ."

"Well, thanks, Danny—for predicting my fun-filled future!" Josh snapped.

"I'm going for help!" Danny said. And, although he hated to leave his twin, he turned and sped away through the water as fast as he could. And that was very fast. In less than a minute he had reached the beach and was clambering up onto the sand.

And then he realized he had some problems. To start with, all of a sudden he was slow and clumsy and heavy. He couldn't move fast at all on his belly and weird, flippery legs. And, of course, he couldn't shout for help either. What on earth was he going to do? How could he possibly save Josh? As soon as he S.W.I.T.C.H.ed back he could run for help, of course . . . but as soon as he S.W.I.T.C.H.ed back, Josh would be S.W.I.T.C.H.ing too, just seconds later.

Danny's head swam with panic. What on earth was he going to do?

Then he heard a very familiar sound. A yapping sound. High-pitched barking and the scamper of long claws across rock. *Piddle*! He had obviously gotten bored up at the cottage and come down to the beach to find them.

"PIDDLE!" Danny yelled. "COME HERE!"

Of course, nothing much came out. No human would have heard anything. But back in the summer, when he'd been a frog stuck in Piddle's mouth (just about to be squelched between his pet's gooey teeth and hot tongue) Danny had managed to get through to the dog. He knew that as well as vibrations and smells and body language, which so many of the creatures he'd S.W.I.T.C.H.ed into used, there was a strange kind of telepathy going on between animals too.

He tried it now, with all his might, concentrating hard on Piddle's flappy ears as the dog wandered along the rocky bits of the beach.

"PIDDLE!!! PIDDLE!!! HERE, BOY! HERE! COME TO ME! COME TO DANNY!"

To his amazement, Piddle looked up, cocked his black and white head to one side, and then came trotting down the beach. In a few seconds, Danny was getting his face licked by an excitable terrier, who was wondering why one of his masters' voices was coming out of this big weird squashed ball thing with legs and a face. But he was getting used to this kind of thing ever since Josh and

Danny started hanging out with that odd lady from next door.

Now what? Far away along the beach, Danny could make out an orange shape. Could that be Petty Potts in her raincoat? "PIDDLE! GO AND GET PETTY POTTS!" Danny yelled at the dog. Piddle stepped back, cocked his head again, and then looked around the beach, wagging his tail.

"YOU KNOW—PETTY POTTS FROM NEXT DOOR!" Danny yelled, waving a flipper in the direction of Petty. "GET HER OVER HERE! JOSH IS IN DANGER!"

Piddle ran round in a circle and peered at Danny's waving flipper. Then—in a weird pulse of telepathy—these words came back: "Fat lady smells funny?"

"YES! YES! FAT LADY SMELLS FUNNY!" Danny agreed. He knew that Piddle had gotten it right. "She's here on the beach! FIND HER!"

Piddle turned and ran. And all Danny could hope was that he knew where he was going—and he'd get there soon.

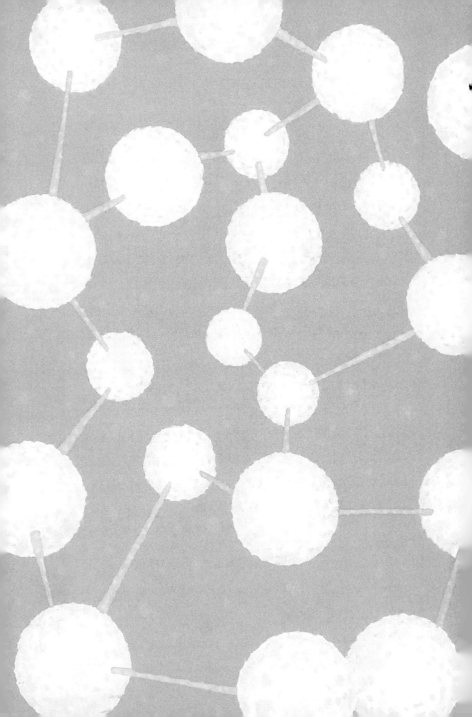

Fat Lady Smells Funny

Petty Potts was ready for some tea. So were Hector and Percy. They'd been S.W.I.T.C.H.ed into turtles three times today, and they'd had enough. Percy was so annoyed that he had tried to bite Petty's bum several times through the pocket he'd been put into, but so far he hadn't managed to gnaw through far enough to get a decent nip in.

"Okey-doke, my brave little helpers," Petty said, glancing up at the steep cliff path. "Scones and cream and jam, I think. Maybe some for you too. What I admire about you both is that, unlike Josh and Danny, you never complain."

Percy paused in mid-gnaw and squeaked, "If you only knew, old woman!" in Mouse.

"I think I have a special empathy for animals, you know," went on Petty.

Across in the other pocket, Hector sat shivering and planning to wee on Petty's scone if he ever got the chance.

"Animals are so much more compliant," Petty said, crouching down and gathering up her bag of scientific bits and pieces, including several spray bottles of S.W.I.T.C.H. and S.W.I.T.C.H. antidote. "No whining and complaining. It's much more restful being around creatures that don't viciously pester me!"

At this point a creature jumped on Petty's head and started to viciously pester her. Piddle yapped furiously in Fat Lady Smells Funny's ear.

"Get OFF me!" Petty shoved the furry missile away and got to her feet, clutching her bag. Piddle kept yapping and began running back and forth, casting urgent glances down to the water.

"What is it, you incontinent animated rug?"

Piddle ran toward the water—and then paused, looked back at Petty, and jerked his head in the direction of the Danny-squashed-ball-with-legs-thingy.

Petty stared after him, her genius brain clicking slowly. Far in the distance she could see a turtle. Perhaps the dog was just excited by this—a genuine leatherback up on the beach.

She squinted and shoved her spectacles up her nose. Hang on . . . genuine leatherbacks didn't usually wave at you, did they?

"OH HO!" she chortled. "Someone's been very naughty, hasn't he?"

She followed Piddle and got ready to give the leatherback a severe talking-to. It would serve

Josh or Danny (whichever one it was) right if that little glitch in the turtle formula *did* happen this time!

She stood over the turtle and put her hands on her hips. "Oh dear, Danny! Or Josh! Got in a bit of a flap, have we?" She smirked.

The turtle made a rather rude gesture at her. And then it pointed out to sea and and waggled its head in an anxious way.

"What are you trying to tell me?" she asked, kneeling down on the sand.

Piddle started yapping again. "Oh, do be quiet, you weak-bladdered ball of fluff!" she snapped. "I don't speak Dog any better than I speak Turtle!" She grabbed her bag. "But this should help us out!" And she pulled out a small bottle of antidote spray and fired it at the turtle. Three seconds later Danny stood in front of her, still flapping his arms about in a frenzy.

"Ah," Petty said, eyeing him with concern. "I thought so. Well—it can't be helped. If you *will* steal my REPTOSWITCH and help yourselves when I have expressly forbidden it, this is what happens!"

"JOSH! JOSH IS OUT THERE!" Danny yelled, ignoring the funny look Petty was giving him. "He's TRAPPED! He's stuck in some fishing net! And he's going to S.W.I.T.C.H. back at ANY time!"

Now Petty did look alarmed. But she rifled through her bag again, extracted a large pair of scissors, and said, "*Where?*"

Danny began to run back into the water, but now he was freaking out over a whole new problem. He could find Josh—the top part of the rocks he was snagged to just showed though the fast incoming tide—and it wasn't that far away. But he was quite deep in the water now—the tide had come in even more! And how would he be able to get down and hold his breath and see what he was doing while he scissored Josh out of danger?

"WAIT!" Petty yelled, running into the shallows behind him. "You'll need this too!" She was holding . . . *a snorkel*!

"PETTY! You are AMAZING!" Danny yelled. He grabbed the snorkel, snapped the plastic face mask over his eyes and nose and shoved the breathing bit into his mouth (trying hard not to think about Petty using it herself during that day's rock pool research). Then he ran into the water, Piddle at his heels. As soon as he was deep enough, he dived under, heading back to Josh, swimming harder and better than he ever had in his life, even with his shorts and T-shirt slowing him down.

He desperately hoped he wasn't too late . . .

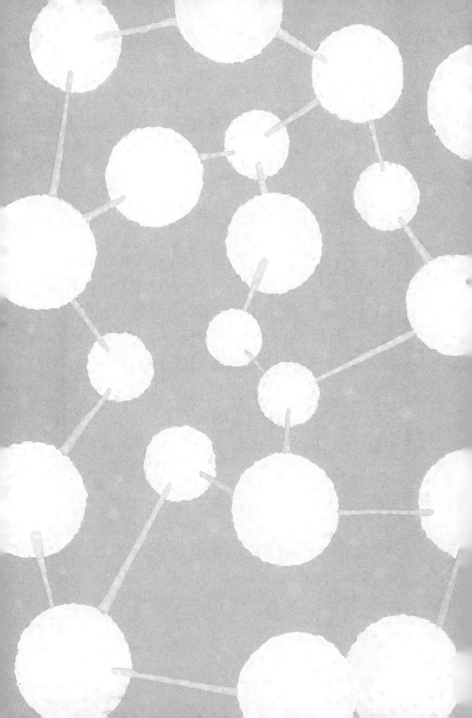

The Rocky Horror Show

As if being trapped in a fishing net along with several other sea-life corpses wasn't bad enough, Josh was now fearing for his shell. The incoming waves were getting more and more lively and kept cracking him against the rocks, first dragging him away as far as the firmly anchored net would allow and then smacking him back again.

If he'd been another kind of turtle, this might not have been such a problem, but Josh knew quite a lot about leatherbacks. As the name suggested, their shells were softer than those of other kinds of turtle. Other kinds had shells with horny scales which acted like armour plating, but the leatherback was designed for speed and top hydrodynamics. It was the fastest turtle on the planet—a kind of sea-going reptilian Ferrari. Its bodywork was beautiful—but not so strong. He knew that eventually his shell would split if he kept being thrown against these jagged rocks.

And if he didn't drown first. He was beginning to feel the need to get some more air. It wasn't desperate yet, but his panicky heart was thrumming away inside his pale flat chest and surely using up more oxygen because of it.

"Bad luck, mate." A spidery figure climbed elegantly and sure-footedly across the rocks beside him. "Nearly got me, that did. I had to use these!" And he raised his fabulous claws.

"Can you get me out?" Josh begged, dimly aware that he was negotiating with a crab—possibly the same one he'd picked up a couple of hours ago. "Snip-snip?"

"Sorry, mate," went on the crab. "You're too snarled up. It'd take me all day, and let's face it—you 'aven't got that long." And he went on his way, his little flickery mouth parts waving regretfully.

Josh pleaded, "You could try . . . !" But the crab didn't come back. Things didn't get much worse, he reflected, than feebly begging for help from a saltwater crustacean.

And then things did get much worse.

There was a powerful thump in the water around him, and all of a sudden the net was biting hard into his skin. He had S.W.I.T.C.H.ed back into boy form! A moment ago he might have had five minutes of air. Now he had thirty seconds.

Josh wriggled desperately, trying to reach his pocket. He could feel that the S.W.I.T.C.H. spray bottle was still in there, and it had to be worth trying to get some of it on his skin, so he could turn turtle again and have a few more minutes. He could spray it right into his mouth. That would work, wouldn't it?

But he just couldn't reach his pocket. His hands were too tightly snagged in the net. In his mind, Josh sighed. Now he *really* knew what it was like to be a leatherback turtle—or a dolphin or a porpoise. Thousands of aquatic reptiles and mammals died in fishing nets every year. He was just about to join the sad tally.

Then he felt something clawing at his arm. He looked around, his mouth clenched shut and his heart hammering, and saw . . . PIDDLE! His dog was scrabbling and biting at the net, his furry snout sending a plume of bubbles as he struggled to stay down underwater and help.

And just behind Piddle was . . . DANNY! Danny as a boy, with a snorkel and—A BIG PAIR OF SCISSORS.

Danny began hacking at the net, After what seemed like an eternity, just as Josh thought his lungs were going to explode, he was pulled free and shot up to the surface of the water. He burst through it and expelled all the dead air inside him in a cough before dragging in a huge, rasping breath.

Struggling to stay above the waves, his feet sliding against the rocky outcrop he'd been trapped on, Josh breathed and breathed and breathed—in spite of Piddle doggy-paddling around him and trying to lick his face.

Then Danny grabbed his arm and helped him swim back to the shore, which wasn't that far. Over the past few minutes, it had felt to Josh as if it was ten miles away.

The twins collapsed onto the beach and lay gasping, staring up into the late afternoon sun.

"All right now, are we?" asked Petty Potts, looming over them and blocking out the light.

"Yes . . ." puffed Danny. "Thanks . . . Petty. I'd . . . never . . . have done it . . . without you!"

"Well, not for the first time," Petty said, crisply. "And I think I'll have this back now, thank you!" She reached into Josh's soaked shorts pocket and retrieved the turtle REPTOSWITCH spray.

"Oh, and what's this?" Petty stood up, holding something else that had come out of Josh's pocket with the spray bottle—a small black fabric bag. She opened it and peered inside.

"A marble . . ." she said. "Not much of a collection, Josh. One marble."

Danny and Josh sat up and stared at each other. To begin with, they stared at each other because they realized the time had come to tell Petty about the Mystery Marble Sender. But they carried on staring at each other for a completely different reason.

"There's a note too," Petty said. "But it's all blurry. Seawater and ink don't go well together."

"Do I look like that?" Josh asked, peering hard at Danny's chest. His T-shirt had been ripped open, and his chest was . . . different.

Danny glanced down and then back at Josh, whose dripping T-shirt was also half hanging off him. "Yup," he said. "Mom and Dad are going to turtle-y freak when they see us!"

They both had pale milky scales all over their chests—and across their bellies—and darker brown and gray scales across their shoulders.

"Yes," Petty said, still gazing at the green marble. "There's a glitch in the REPTOSWITCH formula. I would have told you about it when you came to the lab next week. I thought it was just the chameleon formula. Remember when you were S.W.I.T.C.H.ed back half-chameleon, half-boy a couple of weeks ago? Well, it seems it's not just that REPTOSWITCH that has been affected. Hector and Percy are having the same problem with turtle REPTOSWITCH."

And she fished out the two mice by their tails. They looked very, very put out. And scaly.

"How long until this wears off?" Danny sighed. It had been like this with AMPHISWITCH too.

They'd ended up with frogs' legs for nearly a whole day after they should have properly S.W.I.T.C.H.ed back.

Petty sprayed their scaly areas with more antidote spray. "It will have all gone by tomorrow morning," she said. "Just don't run around in your undies until then!"

And she put all her bottles and the snorkel and the scissors in her bag and started back along the beach.

"Hey—wait!" Josh called. "You've got our marble!"

"Oh—it's lost in my bag now," Petty called back. "I'll dig it out for you later."

"But . . . it's a SPECIAL one!" Danny yelled, as they hurried after her.

Petty turned round and looked at them.

"I know," she said, raising one of her shaggy gray eyebrows. "I made it."

Josh and Danny gaped at her.

"Not a word!" she yelled back, turning away and walking on up the cliff path. "I will see you next week in my lab. We'll have a game of marbles then . . ."

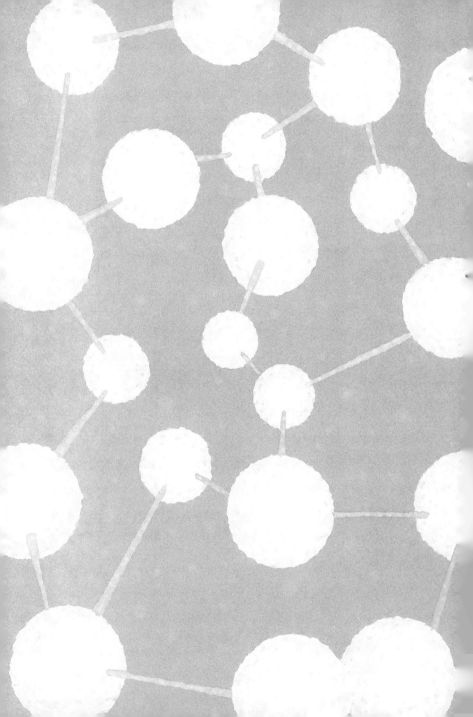

The Scales of Justice

"Josh, Danny! Look—Dad's found a hot tub! We've been heating it up!" Mom said as they climbed wearily into the cottage garden with Piddle at their heels. They were bruised and whacked and in need of big cups of tea and even bigger slices of cake.

"What have you both been up to?" Mom asked, suddenly noticing. "Look at the state of you!"

"We fell in a rock pool," Danny said. It was sort of true.

"And the T-shirts?" Mom asked, raising an eyebrow.

"Sorry," Josh said. "Things got a bit . . . scrapey."

Dad pulled the wooden cover off the big round tub. Underneath, the clear, clean water was steaming and bubbling and looked wonderful. Mom was too cheerful to be cross with them. "Well, why don't you strip off and jump in while I make tea for us all?" she suggested.

Danny and Josh exchanged woeful looks. Suddenly, there was nothing they wanted more than to have a dip in the inviting warm bubbles and ease away the aches and pains brought on by their latest S.W.I.T.C.H. adventure. But they couldn't. Not unless their parents had always *wanted* scaly semi-reptilian sons and never thought to tell them.

"Erm . . . maybe later," Josh said, pulling his T-shirt close around his neck. "I think we need a quick shower—we're all mucky from the beach."

"Yeah . . ." Danny said. "We'll clog up the filter with sand."

"Oh, well—we'll have a go then, shall we?" Mom beamed at Dad. And three seconds later their parents, wearing swimming gear, were happily bobbing up and down in the bubbly water.

"Tea soon," called out Mom. "And I'll tell you what—how about some shellfish for supper?"

"NO SHELLS!" Josh yelled.

Danny added, "ABSOLUTELY NO SHELLS— PLEASE!"

Top Secret!

For Petty Potts's Eyes Only!!

DIARY ENTRY 682.3

SUBJECT: TURTLE-Y UNEXPECTED!

Well, of all the weird coincidences! There I am, innocently experimenting with Turtle REPTOSWITCH, when Josh and Danny show up on my beach!

Of course, I knew they were on holiday in Cornwall, and that's actually what gave me the idea to go down there and try the turtle spray, so I could see how Hector and Percy got on in a big rock pool. But I really had no idea that I had chosen the very same beach on which my young assistants would be holidaying.

Lucky for them that I hung around long enough to rescue Josh from that fishing net after his sneaky S.W.I.T.C.H. into a leatherback turtle. He'd be a goner for sure if it hadn't been for me. I'm really quite heroic at times. There'll be a marble statue of me somewhere, someday . . . But still—to find them on the same beach. Most bizarre.

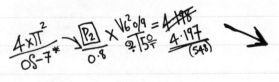 

The REPTOSWITCH is bizarre too. The side effects are a little perplexing. I hope Josh and Danny's parents don't notice the scales before they've faded. A trip to the local doctor would really put the cat among the pigeons. The boys would end up on a freak show—probably that ghastly Destiny Darcy one on Chatz TV!

But even more bizarre than all of this . . . is the marble I discovered in Josh's pocket. It looks like a perfectly ordinary green glass marble. So why does it mean something? What made me say that I had made it? Josh and Danny looked at me as if they thought I'd gone insane.

Why would I make a marble? Perhaps for the same reason that I made the S.W.I.T.C.H. cubes . . . Could there be another code inside this marble? Did I make a whole other set of them? After my backstabbing former friend Victor Crouch burnt out so many bits of my memory, I just can't be sure.

Ah well—I'll find out soon. Time to eat my Cornish cream tea now. Hector and Percy can have a bit too, for their help today.

Hmmm . . . That scone tastes a bit funny . . .

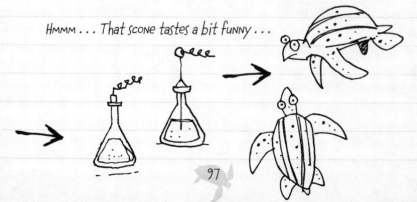

97

GLOSSARY

amphibian: an animal that can live on land and in water

anemone: a sea creature with short tentacles around its mouth

antidote: something that takes away the bad effects of a poison or disease

arachnid: a member of the group of animals that includes spiders and scorpions

cellular: made of cells

crustacean: a shellfish

hijack: to take control of something by force

hologram: a type of photograph made by laser beams. A hologram appears to have depth as well as height and width

mammal: any animal of which the female gives birth to live young and can feed them with her own milk

myriads: a huge number of people or things

predator: an animal that hunts other animals

prey: an animal that is hunted by another animal

reptile: a cold-blooded animal that creeps or crawls, such as lizards and snakes

scales: the thin, overlapping parts on the outside of fish, snakes, and other animals

serum: a kind of fluid used in science and for medical purposes

snout: the front part sticking out from an animal's head, with its nose and mouth

telepathy: communication of thoughts from one person's mind to another without speaking, writing, or gestures

transparent: something is transparent when you can see through it

Recommended Reading

BOOKS

Want to brush up on your reptile knowledge?
Here's a list of books dedicated to creepy-crawlies.

Johnson, Jinny. *Animal Planet™ Wild World: An Encyclopedia of Animals.* Minneapolis: Millbrook Press, 2013.

McCarthy, Colin. *Reptile.* DK Eyewitness Books. New York: DK Publishing, 2012.

Parker, Steve. *Pond & River.* DK Eyewitness Books. New York: DK Publishing, 2011.

WEBSITES

Find out more about nature and wildlife using the websites below.

National Geographic Kids

http://kids.nationalgeographic.com/kids/
Go to this website to watch videos and read facts about your favorite reptiles and amphibians.

San Diego Zoo Kids

http://kids.sandiegozoo.org/animals
Curious to learn more about some of the coolest-looking reptiles and amphibians? This website has lots of information and stunning pictures of some of Earth's most interesting creatures.

US Fish & Wildlife Service

http://www.nwf.org/wildlife/wildlife-library
/amphibians-reptiles-and-fish.aspx
Want some tips to help you look for wildlife in your own neighborhood? Learn how to identify some slimy creatures and some scaly ones as well.

CHECK OUT ALL OF THE

Spider Stampede

Ant Attack

Fly Frenzy

Crane Fly Crash

Grasshopper Glitch

Beetle Blast

 **TITLES!**

Frog Freakout
by Ali Sparkes · Illustrated by Ross Collins

Newt Nemesis
by Ali Sparkes · Illustrated by Ross Collins

Lizard Loopy
by Ali Sparkes
Illustrated by Ross Collins

Chameleon Chaos
by Ali Sparkes
Illustrated by Ross Collins

Turtle Terror
by Ali Sparkes · Illustrated by Ross Collins

Gecko Gladiator
by Ali Sparkes · Illustrated by Ross Collins

Anaconda Adventure
by Ali Sparkes · Illustrated by Ross Collins

Alligator Action
by Ali Sparkes · Illustrated by Ross Collins

About the Author

Ali Sparkes grew up in the wilds of the New Forest, raised by sand lizards who taught her the secret language of reptiles and how to lick her own eyes.

At least, that's how Ali remembers it. Her family argues that she grew up in a house in Southampton, raised by her mom and dad, who taught her the not terribly secret language of English and wished she'd stop chewing her hair.

She once caught a slow worm. It flicked around like mad, and she was a bit scared and dropped it.

Ali still lives in Southampton, now with her husband and two sons. She likes to hang out in the nearby wildlife center spying on common lizards. The lizards are considering legal action . . .

About the Illustrator

Ross Collins's more than eighty picture books and books for young readers have appeared in print around the world. He lives in Scotland and, in his spare time, enjoys leaning backward precariously in his chair.